•Lots to Love•

·LOtS tO LOVe·

AMY BUrrell

VULPINE
PRESS

Published by Vulpine Press in the United Kingdom in 2024

Illustrations by Chuck Harrison

ISBN: 978-1-83919-651-5

www.vulpine-press.com

I would like to dedicate my first published writing to my husband who has always been my biggest supporter and motivator, and who believed in me, before I believed in myself. For that, I will be forever grateful.

Lots to Love about Charlie

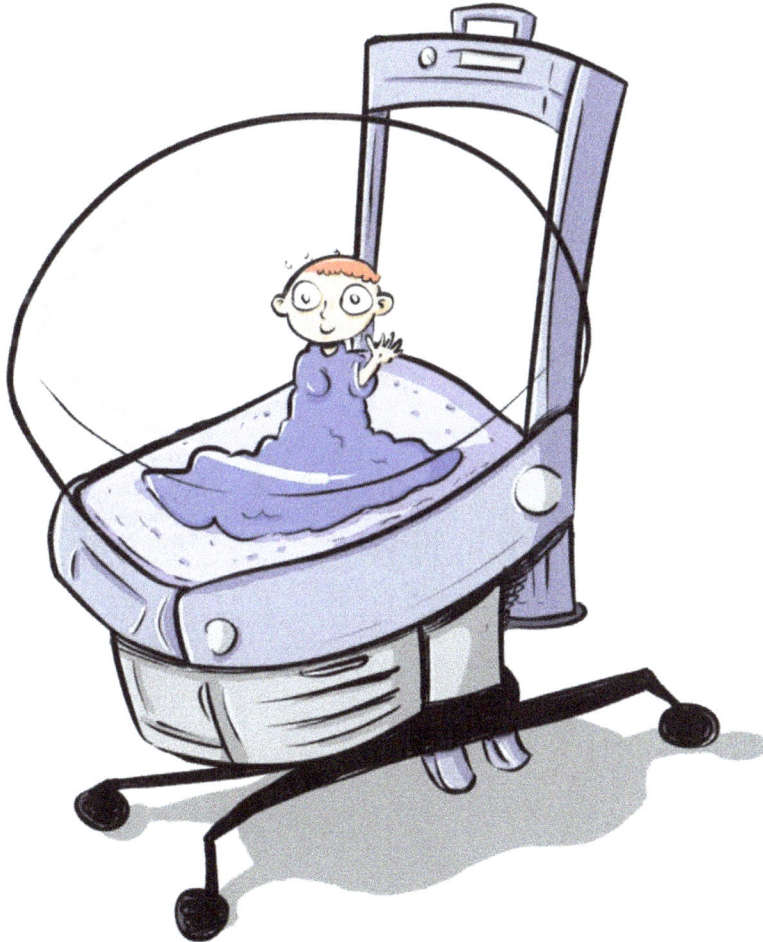

My name is Charlie James

I'm what they call a "Preemie."

Because I couldn't wait so,

From my mommy's tummy I said, "Free Me!"

Being a Preemie means

I came into the world far too soon.

I was born in April,

When I should have been born in June.

Because I was born so early

I am a little bit small

And I had to stay for six whole weeks,

In the safe warm hospital

I slept in an incubator,

Which is a cot that keeps me warm,

And they kept me in there safe and sound,

Until the day I should have been born.

They kept me warm; they kept me safe,

And I was not alone,

There were lots of babies in there,

All just waiting to go home.

We all had different needs,

Some babies were more poorly than others.

But what we all really loved was

Seeing our parents, sisters, and brothers!

I have bright big eyes,

Little fingers and curly hair,

And everyone says I'm special,

Because Preemie babies are very rare.

I am still a little baby and

I've only just made it home.

I don't know what I will want to do,

Once I'm all big and grown.

My mommy and daddy say,

I can do anything, it's up to me,

But I'm too little yet,

To have any great big dreams.

One day when I am older,

I will make my choice,

But for now, I laugh and cry and scream,

As I discover my voice.

My name is Charlie James and,

There's lots to love about me,

Because one day when I'm older

I will chase down all my dreams.

Lots to Love about Lottie

My name is Lottie Pickles,

And I have restricted growth.

My brother's name is Peter,

And it affects us both.

When we go to the park,

I can't run that fast

And when we're in P.E.,

They always pick me last.

I like to play basketball,

But it's hard when I'm so small,

Peter struggles with it, too,

Even though he's in big school.

Some people call us dwarves,

And that's okay with me.

But Peter doesn't like it much,

So, we just call him Pete.

I'm not very tall at all,

So, it's hard to reach up high,

But I know I will do it one day,

If I find the right thing to climb.

I really love to run,

But I'm a little wobbly on my feet.

And I'm okay with that,

Because mom told me about para-athletes.

Para-athletes are amazing,

They are sports people just like me,

They achieve incredible sporting things,

With all types of ability.

Lottie and Peter Pickles,

That's what it says on our school badges.

And our mom says she loves us because,

All the best things come in small packages.

My name is Lottie Pickles,

And there's lots to love about me,

My superpower is being a little bit small,

And one day I'll be a para-athlete.

LOTS TO LOVE ABOUT RUPERT

My name is Rupert,

And I am hard of hearing.

So, I wear a hearing aid,

That looks just like an earring.

Sometimes when you talk,

I have to read your lips,

And sometimes when I talk,

I use my fingertips.

I can talk in Sign Language,

It's like a secret code,

My mom and dad learned a bit,

But my teacher knows the most.

I like to use my hands to talk,

Because it's easier for me to see,

And because I use my hands so much,

I always keep them clean.

I keep my hands clean in the kitchen,

When I help my dad bake a cake,

But a winter stew with my mom;

That's really my favourite thing to make.

I don't always hear the oven alarm,

When it tells you the food is cooked,

So, Mom or Dad will wave their hands,

So I know to have a look!

I'd like to be a Head Chef,

But I'll start as a line or a sous,

I'll make lots of yummy creations,

Like my favourite, my mom's stew…

My name is Rupert Round,

And I'm a little bit deaf,

And there's lots to love about me,

One day I'll be an award-winning chef!

Lots to Love about Cora

My name is Cora Cotton

And I was born unable to swallow.

But I have a feeding tube,

That stops my belly from feeling hollow.

My tube goes up my nose,

And down into my tummy

To give me all my food

And tell me what is yummy.

I do not chew my food,

And I can't tell how it tastes,

It all runs through my tube,

Like how water runs in lakes.

One day when I'm older,

I think I'd like to be a nurse,

So, I can help children with tubes

And tell them, "It really doesn't hurt!"

I think I'd be quite good at it.

A nurse must be caring and kind.

And when a child is scared of having a tube,

I can say, "Look, I just love mine!"

My tube has made me healthy,

It's helped me eat and made me grow,

Your tube will help you, too,

And you'll know you're not alone.

My name is Cora Cotton,

And I have a feeding tube to help me eat.

And there's lots to love about me,

One day I'll be a nurse, rushed right off my feet!

Lots to Love about Birio

My name is Birio Singh

And I have something called ASD

That stands for Autism Spectrum Disorder

And it has lots of effects on me.

My ASD means that I can struggle,

With new people or to be in a new place,

So sometimes I need my mom to help me stim,

And sometimes I just need my own space.

Sometimes I need extra help,

Learning what is safe,

And when I have my dinner,

I separate all my food on my plate.

I don't like mixing colours,

And the textures can be weird,

I love to hug my safe people,

But never anyone with a beard.

I can get a bit overwhelmed;

With lots of smells and big bright colours

But that doesn't mean that I can't do

The same as my sisters and my brothers.

I like to learn about religions,

My mom has taught me lots.

I'm not the best with English and maths,

But I can tie many different knots.

I am a Cub Scout now,

Before that I did Beavers,

And when I am all grown up

I want to be the best Scout Leader

At Scouts I learn about so many things

They teach lots of practical skills

I even started camping with them,

And I just think it is brill!

I never thought I'd be able to be away,

From my mom for a whole night,

But because I feel safe at scouts

I didn't have a fright.

ASD is a condition that can

Affect different people in different ways,

Like how I'm very chatty,

But my friend Ella can struggle with what she says,

I can't tell you how ASD might affect someone else,

I can only say how it affects me,

But I have learned it's a superpower

And I have skills that others don't see.

My name is Birio Singh

And there's lots to love about me,

When I'm big I'll be a Scout Leader

And help other children with ASD.

Lots to Love about Kiki

My name is Kiki Coddington

And I have type 1 diabetes

Sometimes I need healthy foods

And sometimes I just need sweeties

Diabetes means my body

Can't control the sugar in my blood

So sometimes there's not enough,

And sometimes there's far too much.

I have this condition because

My body can't make insulin,

That's something already in most bodies

But I have to inject it in.

Sometimes I get very tired

And sometimes I feel quite slow

This can be because

My sugars are very low

Sometimes I can feel very hyper

And I really just can't sit still

And this can be because

my sugars are as high as a great big hill

We have to check my sugars

With this special machine,

We prick my finger and test the blood

And wait for the numbers on the screen

We have to watch carefully

To see what numbers it might show

Because I can be very poorly

If my sugars go too high or too low.

I used to be afraid of needles

But now I do my own tests

And honestly, I'm not scared anymore

Because I take blood the best.

One day when I'm older,

I'll use all the practise I've gained,

To become a phlebotomist

And help others who might be afraid.

A phlebotomist works in a hospital

And they take people's blood

To find out what is wrong with them,

And look at what's bad or good.

When I have my job, when I'm all grown up,

I'll help work out what's wrong,

And if someone is afraid of needles,

I'll distract them by singing a song.

My name is Kiki Coddington

And there's lots to love about me,

One day I'll be a phlebotomist,

And I'll help others with diabetes.

LOTS TO LOVE ABOUT KIP

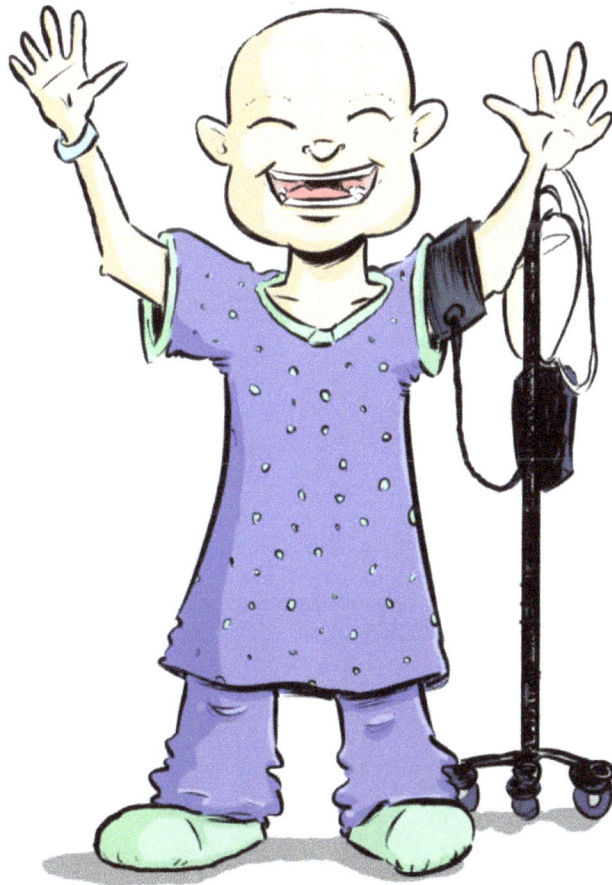

My name is Kip Curtis,

And I have Leukaemia

This can cause lots of problems,

Like tiredness and anaemia.

I know these are super big words,

And I struggled with them so much,

But Leukaemia is a type of cancer,

That lives inside my blood.

Your blood is made up of lots of cells

Some are red and some are white

In order to stay healthy

They need to balance each other just right.

Leukaemia means my body is making

Too many broken white blood cells

So, I feel very tired, hot and chilly,

And really just very unwell.

Anaemia means your body,

Doesn't have enough red blood cells,

This means I may go pale or moody,

And I have a lot of dizzy spells.

My illness makes me very sick,

And there is no easy fix,

I spend lots of time in hospital

And I might be stuck like this.

Going to hospital all the time

Is really not much fun,

But on the way with Mom and dad

There's a tunnel where I run.

And in the tunnel, I shout and shout

Even when I'm losing hope,

Mom and Dad let me say naughty words

Just to help me cope

"SMELLY PANTS WEE!

STINKY PANTS STINKY!

TOILET BOWL STINK AND

SMELLY PANTS WEE!"

My dad recorded me once,

And sent the clip into a radio show,

And now I hear "SMELLY PANTS WEE"

Everywhere I seem to go.

I am feeling very poorly,

I am very tired, and I've lost all my hair,

But even though I'm only 5 years old,

It's clear to see how much I care.

Because of all I've been through,

And thinking of others who are poor,

We started up a fundraiser,

And are collecting more and more.

We are raising lots of money.

To send to children just like me

Who have very bad illnesses

But no hospital or money.

I may not live forever,

But my name will always live on,

The money I raised will help children

For years and years to come.

My name is Kip Curtis

And there's lots to love about me,

So, when you're feeling down and out,

Just give a great big shout of… "SMELLY PANTS WEE!"

About Kip Curtis

The story about Kip Curtis is a story of a real boy who lived a far too short life. Kip's passing left parents Ed and Sarah, sister Millie, and new brother Arlo to learn to navigate life in the most impossible circumstances.

Their strength as a family has been indescribable and they have, to date, raised over £45,000 for various cancer charities, with their primary focus of donations now being on World Child Cancer UK (Registered charity number: 1084729). If any of the stories in this book have inspired, entertained, or resonated with you, please consider making a donation in honour of Kip and do shout "SMELLY PANTS WEE!" at any opportunity you find for silliness in life, especially in the face of fear.

Thank you so much.

Acknowledgements

My acknowledgements and appreciation go to all the incredible real people these characters have been inspired by, including the families of those who have been gracious enough to encourage my writing about their loved ones. My heartfelt thanks to all.

I would also like to remember my two grandfathers who helped me learn to jump the hurdles life throws at me and who have sadly passed before meeting my child, seeing me wed, or reading my stories, may they live on in my memories and in this print.

I would like to dedicate 'Lots to Love about Charlie' to my very own preemie baby Charlie James, who arrived in 2021 and has changed my life exponentially for the better.

Amy Burrell is a young writer who has dealt with disability in her own life, and has been inspired by her lived experiences working with children and young people in both professional and voluntary roles for well over a decade. Amy was born and raised in Birmingham, England, and volunteers to run a community youth group where she has been surrounded by great cultures, amazing people, and incredible stories all her life.